BE
DO NOT
BOOK FROM
BEGINNING TO END!

Can't sleep? No wonder — you're in the creepiest old inn you've ever seen. You just know this place is going to give you nightmares.

But there's something you *don't* know. In this place, your nightmares can come true! Especially if they involve the terrifying Sleep Master. If you don't handle him right, he could turn your parents into aliens — or turn *you* into a bat! Can you take control of your dreams — or will you be trapped in a nightmare forever?

This scary adventure is about *you.* You decide what will happen — and how terrifying the scares will be!

Start on page 1. Then follow the instructions at the bottom of each page. You make the choices. If you choose well, you might even end up rich and famous! But if you make the wrong choice . . . BEWARE!

SO TAKE A DEEP BREATH. CROSS YOUR FINGERS. AND TURN TO PAGE 1 TO *GIVE YOURSELF GOOSEBUMPS*!

READER BEWARE —
YOU CHOOSE THE SCARE!

Look for more
GIVE YOURSELF GOOSEBUMPS adventures
from R.L. STINE:

R.L. STINE

GIVE YOURSELF Goosebumps®

IT'S ONLY A NIGHTMARE!

AN
APPLE
PAPERBACK

SCHOLASTIC INC.
New York Toronto London Auckland Sydney

A PARACHUTE PRESS BOOK

ISBN 0-590-76785-2

12 11 10 9 8 7 6 5 4 3 2 1 8 9/9 0 1 2 3/0

Printed in the U.S.A. 40

First Scholastic printing, December 1998

Hurry! you urge yourself. Run faster!

You're running for your life down a long, dark hallway. A huge, smelly, terrifying *something* is right behind you. But it's as if you're running in quicksand! Your legs churn — but you don't go anywhere. You try to scream — but nothing comes out.

You hear the thing's hooves clatter on the wood floor. You feel its hot breath on the back of your neck.

It's so close!

Suddenly you're on the roof. How did you get *there*?

But the thing is still after you!

Tentacles wrap around your ankle. "Oh, no!" you scream. You turn and kick like a maniac. As hard as you can.

You did it! You broke free!

But the force of your kick sends you backwards. You teeter at the edge of the roof.

"Aaaaaaah!" you shriek. You fall into the dark void. This is the end!

But the fall seems to go on forever. And with each passing second your terror grows.

Drop to PAGE 2.

"Oh, no!"

You jerk yourself upright, shaking. Your T-shirt is soaked with cold sweat.

"Not another nightmare!" you moan. With a trembling hand, you reach for the lamp by your bed and switch it on.

As light floods the room, it all comes rushing back to you. That's right. You're on vacation with your parents and you're sleeping at an inn. Your folks are snoring in the next room.

You grab the quilt and tuck it under your chin. Be calm, you tell yourself.

Your mom and dad love this inn. They think it's "quaint." You think it's old and creaky. The place gives you the creeps.

Was that a sound? Nervously, you glance behind you. You gasp.

The hideous, distorted face of a gargoyle is only inches away!

Gape at the gargoyle on PAGE 3.

In another second you realize the truth. The gargoyle is only a wooden carving. Part of the headboard of your bed.

It isn't real, you reassure yourself.

There are four gargoyles carved into the headboard. Their mouths are open in ghastly grins. Their claws seem to dig into the headboard. Their wings are spread as if ready to take flight.

No wonder you had a nightmare!

You edge away from the headboard toward the middle of the bed. You hate nightmares more than anything. The worst are the ones with the Sleep Master.

The Sleep Master is a strange character who appears often in your nightmares. Sometimes he looks like a kid your age. Sometimes you can't even see his face. But his eyes are always the same — gray and cold. And he always says the same thing: "Wake up! Your whole life is a dream. What you call the dream world is the reality. Wake up and live it!"

The Sleep Master scares you more than any gargoyle. You have the feeling that if he catches you in your dream, you'll never wake up.

But of course, the Sleep Master is only a dream.

Isn't he?

Go to PAGE 4.

You shiver as you think about the Sleep Master. Now you'll *never* fall back to sleep.

The clock on the nightstand says it's only 1 A.M. You can't stay up all night. Tomorrow morning, you and your folks are supposed to go on a hike. You've got to get some sleep!

But you don't want to stretch out under those gargoyles.

You could wake up your parents — but only little kids do that. Besides, they'd tell you it was a dream and to go back to sleep.

You could go downstairs to the kitchen of the inn and find something to eat. But the dark old house is just as scary as the bed.

So what do you do?

If you go downstairs, go to PAGE 63.
If you try to sleep in the bed, go to PAGE 122.

The Sleep Master opens fire again.

"I'm out of here!" you cry, and hit the EJECT button.

KABOOM!

Your seat blasts out of the cockpit just before the rocket disintegrates your jet.

"Sucker!" You gloat. Now all you have to do is wait for your parachute to open.

As you wait, you notice something bad.

Very bad.

You're not wearing a parachute!

The ground rushes up to meet you. Your stomach twists with the sickening feeling of falling. You brace yourself for the deadly impact. But the impact doesn't come.

You force yourself to peer down. Huh? Though you're dropping fast, the ground isn't coming any closer. You must be going a hundred miles an hour. But you just fall and fall.

"Wake up!" you shout at yourself. But you can't wake up. And every moment, you feel the same terrible fear and panic.

Bad luck! You're stuck in a nightmare that will never

END.

6

The doctor seems very smart. He must know what he's talking about. "All right," you agree. "Let's try it."

"I'm happy," the doctor begins.

"I'm sad," you shoot back.

"It's daytime," he says.

You grin. "It's nighttime." This is easy!

"This is a dream." The doctor's voice is soothing.

"This is real," you reply without thinking.

In a flash, the psychoanalyst is gone. In his chair sits the Sleep Master. And he's wearing a tweed suit.

"You tricked me!" you cry.

"I had to," he apologizes. "I had to get you to face reality — this reality. Now you're cured. You never have to worry about going back to that boring world again."

"You mean, I'm trapped here?" you wail.

"Forever!" the Sleep Master confirms.

By saying the wrong words, you've trapped yourself permanently in your own dreams!

"But I have to get home!" you protest.

"You are home," the Sleep Master says. "Isn't it wonderful?"

"Yeah," you moan. "It's a real dream come true!"

THE END

"The army awaits your command," the Sleep Master says fiercely.

Rising in your saddle, you draw your bright steel sword. You turn to your army and scream at the top of your lungs.

"CHARGE!"

Then you spur your steed straight at the enemy. Your excitement grows. You turn to urge your troops on.

Hey! Where are your troops?

Looking back, you see your army far behind you. They haven't moved!

"Come on!" you scream. "Charge! Advance!"

But they don't move. With a jolt of fear you realize what has happened.

Lord Morphos has made your army deaf! They can't hear you! None of them heard your command to charge!

"Whoa!" you shout to your steed. But it doesn't hear you, either! It keeps galloping forward. It's just you against ten thousand enemy soldiers. You don't have a chance!

You turn to your troops. You wonder if they can read your lips:

"HELLLLLLLLP!"

THE END

You wake up with a start.

I must have dozed off, you think. You lift your head from the damp, muddy forest floor. What a strange dream!

Ferns line the banks of a nearby stream. They keep the ground nice and cool, just the way you like it. You raise yourself on all four legs — until you're a quarter inch off the ground. You begin to slither through the mud.

I dreamed I was a kid who dreamed he was a dragon, you think in amazement.

As you slide into the cool, clear water, you say to yourself, Wait till the other salamanders hear about this!

THE END

You reach out to shake your mom's arm. But then you draw your hand away.

No, you say to yourself. I can't. What if waking them up traps them in this dream world with me?

Still, you can't bear to leave your folks — not yet. You gaze down at them. Their faces are so comforting and —

Terrifying!

As you watch, your parents' heads swell. Soon they look like huge, pale eggs. Their eyes grow to the size of grapefruits. Their hair falls out, and their heads turn bald and shiny. Their arms grow long and thin as matchsticks.

You hold your breath, too scared to run. What's happening to them?

Then both your parents open their eyes at exactly the same moment. Except their eyes are solid red disks!

It hits you like a ton of bricks.

Your parents have turned into aliens from outer space!

Go to PAGE 72.

10

You reach out and press FAST FORWARD.

With a blur of motion, the "you" on the TV screen tosses and turns in his sleep. In a few seconds, a whole night goes by.

It's working, you think. I'm going to see the future.

On TV, the first rays of dawn appear through the windows. You watch your eyes open. You're awake!

"I did it!" you cry. "I woke up! This tape shows the future. So I'm definitely going to wake up tomorrow morning. And this dream will be over!"

"Sorry," someone says.

You spin around and come face-to-face with the Sleep Master. Now he's dressed in a tweed suit, like the psychoanalyst.

"What do you want?" you shout at him.

"To congratulate you," he replies with a smile.

On what? Find out on PAGE 112.

11

You can't believe it — you won the marathon. *And* you're a billionaire! The next thing you know, you're standing in front of a huge crowd of people, making a speech.

"And that's why you should elect me president!" you declare.

The crowd goes wild, chanting your name. They pick you up and carry you on their shoulders. Now you're in Washington, D.C., being carried to the White House.

"Hey!" you shout. "Don't we need an election?"

George Washington greets you at the door. "I cannot tell a lie: We canceled the election," he tells you. "No one wanted to run against you. Oh, and by the way, you have your own show on MTV."

Feeling happy and proud, you walk into the Oval Office. You plop down behind the big oak desk. All you ever wanted has come true.

There is one problem, though — you feel tired from running the marathon.

No big deal, you think. I can take a nap if I want to. After all — I'm president, right?

You put your head down on the desk and zonk out.

Go to PAGE 93.

That dagger is like a toothpick, you think. But I bet the broadsword can cause some major damage. You draw it from its scabbard.

It promptly clunks to the ground. Wow! It's heavy, you think. Still, you're so pumped, you manage to raise the sword high.

"Morphos!" you shout. "Prepare to meet thy doom!" You never had the chance to use the word *thy* before. Cool!

"Come!" Lord Morphos roars, spurring his black steed toward you.

You spur your horse. The two of you wheel about each other, waiting to strike. You see an opening. You thrust.

And promptly shatter your sword against his shield.

Oh, no!

What are you going to do now? Find out on PAGE 88.

You don't know where the Sleep Master went. And you don't really care anymore. You're having too good a time as a horse.

It feels great to trot down the hill toward the other horses. You're excited at the idea of jumping, playing, and eating apples with them.

You're not sure how horses say hi. So you stop a few feet away and paw the ground.

A really cute-looking horse comes up to you. You feel a little shy. How do I break the ice? you wonder.

You never get a chance to find out. The horse suddenly starts morphing into something . . . horrible. Its front hooves become claws. Its mouth fills with a double row of shark's teeth.

You glance at the other horses in terror. Yikes! They're changing too!

Your mane practically stands on end in your fear. You flee from the horse-things, galloping like the wind. But the terrifying animals are chasing you!

You run as if your life depends on it. Because it does.

Gallop to PAGE 44.

A look of anger crosses the Sleep Master's thin face. "I can't get back because of the ruler of this dream world," he replies. "He has trapped me here — and he will do the same to you."

"The ruler?" you stammer. Your brain is being overloaded by too much weirdness. "What ruler?"

"Lord Morphos," the Sleep Master explains. "He rules this dream world. His dream crystal seizes us while we sleep and traps us here. We can only escape by defeating him."

"Defeating him?" you repeat. That sounds dangerous.

"I've been here so long, I've gained some powers," the Sleep Master adds. "I can change the dream a little bit. But Lord Morphos can change the dream any way he wants. I've tried to battle him, but I'm not strong enough by myself. But the two of us might be able to defeat him — if we work together."

Work your way to PAGE 26.

Suddenly you're standing at the head of a long table. A dozen men and women sit in two rows down either side. They're all dressed in business suits.

Everyone is staring at you.

"So what should we do, boss?" the man on your right asks you. "Buy or sell?"

It takes you a moment to figure out what has happened. Then you remember the gargoyles and the bed.

Wow! Your dream is coming true. You're in charge of some giant corporation.

These people must work for you. You're in the middle of a meeting and they're all waiting to hear what you have to say.

The only problem is, you don't know what they're talking about.

"Should we buy or should we sell?" the man asks again.

They're all waiting for an answer. You're the boss. Now you have to make a decision. What will it be?

If you say "buy," go to PAGE 17.
If you say "sell," go to PAGE 58.

A moment later, you're back in the room where the whole mess started. Everything looks the same — the bed, the scary headboard with the gargoyles, the moonlight coming in through the windows. It's hard to believe any of it really happened.

Maybe Mom is right, you think, as you slide into bed. Maybe it all *was* a dream, and I'm awake now.

You lay your head on the pillow.

"Now, stop worrying," your mother coos. "Your dreams can't hurt you. Everything will be all right in the morning."

You feel safe now. You're sure Mom is right. What can a dream do to you, anyway?

You close your eyes. Immediately, you drift off. What a relief it is to finally be able to sleep. . . .

Turn to PAGE 28.

You take a deep breath. "Buy!" you declare.

The executives around the table gaze at you solemnly. No one says anything for several long seconds.

Then the man on your right reaches toward a big red button on the table. You read the label printed underneath.

TRAPDOOR

"Trapdoor?" you ask. "But —"

The executive says, "Your decision to buy has a downside to it."

"What do you mean?" you demand. You're starting to worry.

In answer, the executive presses the button.

Instantly a trapdoor opens under your feet. The next thing you know, you're dropping down a chute from the top of the hundred-story office building. Next stop, the sidewalk.

The sidewalk. That's a definite downside!

Before you go *SPLAT*, you have time to say one word:

"Bye!"

THE END

18

"I didn't dream this!" you shout.

"What's wrong?" your mother asks in a strange voice.

You're too shocked to answer. Your mom has become a real robot! Her skin is polished steel. Her eyes are flashing red lights. Your father stomps into the room on heavy metal feet. He's a robot too!

"No!" you cry. "I said they were *like* robots!"

In your dream, you turned your parents into robots. And since you're their child, *you must be a robot too*!

Already everything below your chest is steel and wires.

"Okay. Okay," you say quickly. "No problem. All I have to do is dream I'm human."

Your computer brain commands your circuits to dream. Nothing happens!

"What's wrong?" crackles your electronic voice. Why can't you dream yourself human?

And then you find out. A message appears on a small computer screen on your arm. Your heart sinks as you read it:

ERROR — ROBOTS DO NOT DREAM.

THE END

You leap off the couch. Just in time to avoid a beam of blazing white light shooting from the vaporizer's arm! The couch you were sitting on disappears with a sizzle.

"Butler!" you yell. "Stop it!"

The butler appears next to you.

"You called?" he asks, very politely. Meanwhile, a laser beam shoots a hole through the wall next to you.

You scramble along the floor, yelling. "This thing is going to clean me to death! Turn it off!"

"I'm sorry," the butler replies sadly. "Only the central computer can override the cleaning program."

"The central computer?" you shout. An energy blast destroys the floor in front of you. "Where's that?"

"I'm not sure," the butler answers. "After all, I'm just the butler, not a computer scientist. Will that be all?"

You don't bother to answer. You're too busy figuring out where the central computer is. Or maybe you should just head for the nearest door and try to escape.

If you head for the door, go to PAGE 47.

If you try to find the central computer, go to PAGE 60.

You dash up the long staircase, grinning. Things are going to turn out okay, you think. Your parents will know what to do. You run to the door of their room and fling it open. Then you stop.

Your mom and dad are there, all right. But they're asleep.

You tiptoe quietly to the side of their bed. Your dad is snoring. Mom is smiling as if she's having a nice dream.

Can people dream in a dream? you wonder. But the most important question is this: Should you wake them or not?

If you do, maybe they'll be able to help you. But what if you wake them up and they get stuck in this insane dream world with you? Can you risk dooming your parents?

You stand there, nervously figuring out what to do.

If you wake your parents, go to PAGE 106.
If you don't wake them, go to PAGE 9.

You gaze at the army gathered around you on the plain. One by one they kneel before you.

"You may return to your dull reality," the Sleep Master explains. "Or, if you wish, remain here in the dream world as its new ruler. Anything you dream will come true."

The Sleep Master adds with a frown, "If you stay, you cannot return to your old reality. You must rule here forever. The dream world awaits your decision."

For a moment, your mind reels at your chance for limitless power.

But it's only power over dreams, you think.

Still, the words of the Sleep Master echo in your mind. *Anything you dream will come true.*

What do you decide?

If you stay to rule over the dream world, go to PAGE 132.

If you go back to reality, go to PAGE 56.

You have to admit: The gargoyles did warn you to be careful. Besides, what harm can a little match do?

You reach out. The dog gargoyle grins and gives you the box. But when you slide it open, it's empty.

"Hey, there aren't any matches in here!" you cry angrily.

"Not in there," the gargoyle says. "Over there." It points to the hole your house fell into.

Except now your house is standing again. "My house!" you gasp.

"Not your house," the dog gargoyle corrects you. "But a perfect *match* for it."

Huh? Well, you don't have time to play word games with this beast. Maybe there's a flashlight in the house.

"Thanks, pooch," you toss over your shoulder. "Hey, if there's anything I can do for you, just let me know."

You run up the front stairs and through the front door.

Go to PAGE 43.

I want to tell off the real principal, you think. You throw open the door to his office.

He looks up from his desk with a big smile.

"There you are!" he gushes. "I'm so glad to see you!"

"You are?" you reply, caught off guard.

"Of course!" he cries, getting up and coming around to you. "This is your big day!"

He ushers you back into the hall.

"Hurry up!" he urges you. "They're about to start."

What's up? Maybe you're going to get an award for being most likely to be good-looking!

The two of you halt in front of a large door.

"Here we are," the principal says in a cheery voice.

"Oh, good!" you gasp, out of breath.

"So get ready," he booms, "for the most important test of your life!"

Take the test on PAGE 129.

You turn to the chapter called "Beautiful Dreamer." This is what you read:

"Imagine you're sinking into a deep feather bed. It's so soft, you could sleep for seventy years. Slowly repeat these words."

You feel a little silly, but you start repeating the words to yourself.

"Hibernate, vegetate, sleep, slumber, doze.
Shut-eye, siesta, snooze, nap, repose."

Before you know it, you start to feel relaxed. Then drowsy. You have trouble repeating the words.

"Shut-eye, semester, shnoz, nab, suppose . . .
. . . *ZZZZZZ* . . ."

Go to PAGE 104.

"Let's play video games," you decide.

Benny nods excitedly. He leads the whole group down the hall.

In this dream there must be a video arcade in school, you muse. Awesome!

You enter the room behind Benny. But instead of rows of video games, you see just one giant screen. On the screen is a chessboard.

"Computer chess?" you blurt out.

"Of course," Benny replies. "I don't play those silly, childish, violent, uneducational arcade games."

You roll your eyes. No wonder Benny has no friends.

Benny points to the screen. "No human has ever beaten this computer. If one of us could do it, we'd be famous!"

You shrug. "No problem! I can do it!"

"Really?" Benny's eyes grow wide.

"Sure," you boast. After all, it's your dream, right?

Nothing to it, you tell yourself, as you sit in front of the giant screen. Just think like a chess piece.

That's the last thing you think before the room vanishes.

Move to PAGE 100.

Your mind reels from the Sleep Master's words. Just a moment ago he was the enemy. Now he's asking you to help him. Can you believe him?

Besides, this is all a dream, isn't it? Why can't you just wake up?

You feel tired and faint. You lean against the low wall that runs around the tower. It feels cold, hard, and very real. Once again you realize this is no ordinary dream. You really are trapped here.

That helps you make up your mind.

"Okay," you tell the Sleep Master. "What do we do?"

"It won't be easy," he cautions. "We have two choices. Either we defeat Lord Morphos in battle, or we challenge him to a contest of wits. Which do you prefer?"

Standing on the stone tower, you think hard.

If you choose battle, go to PAGE 66.
If you choose a contest of wits, go to PAGE 94.

"Very well," says the voice in your brain. "Here is the question. If you answer it, I will send you back to your reality. If you are incorrect, I will keep you here forever."

"Two orangutans in Brazil are trying to cross the Amazon. Their canoe only holds two hundred pounds. One orangutan weighs eighty-nine kilograms. The other is named Edna, but everyone calls her Coco. If it's July fourteenth, how many more minutes will it take a cubic foot of ice to melt than for Coco to eat a banana?

"You have thirty-five seconds," the voice adds.

TICK . . . TICK . . . A loud clock starts ticking.

How can you figure out this crazy problem? It makes no sense.

Think until PAGE 125.

28

The next thing you know, it's morning. You throw off the covers and jump out of bed.

"It really *was* a dream!" you cry. You pull on your clothes and run downstairs to the dining room to join your family. And there they are — your mom, your dad, and —

The Sleep Master!

He's eating pancakes with your parents!

It can't be! But it is. You were still asleep when you woke up your parents. So when you woke them, they became part of the dream world.

"Mom! Dad!" you tell them. "I'm sorry, I didn't mean for this to happen."

"No sweat," assures your dad. "But just because we're in your dream, don't think you can get out of doing chores."

Your mom passes a stack of pancakes to you. "Eat up, dear," she says cheerfully. "Breakfast is the most important meal of any dream!"

"Yes," the Sleep Master agrees. "Eat up. Because if you think you're ever waking up again, you're dreaming!"

THE END

The gorilla gargoyle hops onto the bed and hovers over you. You want to swat the gross thing. But you're afraid to touch it. Afraid of what it might do to you.

"You have to make a choice," it explains.

"A choice of dreams," adds the eyeless gargoyle. "That's the power of the bed. You choose your dreams."

"And you make them come true," the devil chimes in.

"Only," says the gorilla, "be careful what you dream of — it will absolutely, positively come true."

Just chill, you tell yourself. This is only a dream. Any minute now you'll wake up.

Then another thought hits you.

What if it was possible? What if you really *could* make your dreams come true?

Go to PAGE 111.

You start repeating the order into the microphone. But you can't remember what it was. Did he say "hold the mustard"? Or was it "extra cheese"?

You glance down the line. Whoa! There must be fifty people there. They all look hungry and impatient. And they're getting angrier by the second.

You break out in a nervous sweat.

You have to hurry up and place the order. But what should you say?

If you say "hold the mustard," go to PAGE 78.
If you say "extra cheese," turn to PAGE 77.

I'll never pass this test on my own, you think. Besides, it's not fair. No one told me about it.

You grab the paper. Then you feel a tap on your shoulder. It's the principal. He holds out his hand.

"I see you've already completed the test," he says cheerfully. "Let's see how you did."

You don't know what to do. As you stand there, confused, he takes the paper from you.

"Hmmm," he mutters, his face growing clouded. "Hmmm . . ."

"What?" you cry finally, unable to take the suspense.

He looks at you with concern. "I'm afraid you got every answer wrong. You'll have to go back to kindergarten — for the rest of your life!"

Kindergarten?

The next thing you know, you're squeezed into a very small chair with your legs under a very short table. You're in a kindergarten class with five-year-olds.

You raise your hand and ask the teacher, "Is it time for milk and cookies yet?"

THE END

This is my big chance to be popular, you think. You casually walk over to the "in crowd."

"Hey! You're just in time!" says Bobby Smith, the basketball star. "We're going to the cafeteria. We were waiting for you!"

Waiting for me? you think as you all head downstairs. Wow! They like me! They really like me!

The cafeteria is packed with kids. As soon as the cool clique walks in, everyone stares. Kids you don't even know say hello.

It feels great. You always wanted to be liked by everyone. Now you are.

You and your crowd sit together at the best lunch table. This is the greatest, you think as you sit down. Everyone likes me!

"This is the greatest!" Bobby Smith says as he pokes you with a fork. "I really like it!"

Go to PAGE 118.

"How did you get into this hot water?" asks the voice of Lord Morphos.

"I used my noodle!" you shout.

"Did you say *noodle*?"

The next instant Morphos's brain disappears. In its place is a huge mass of spaghetti. Even stranger, the spaghetti begins to talk to you.

"How do you like your noodle?" it demands. "With meat sauce? Tomato sauce? Cream sauce?"

The water is growing hotter and hotter. You're being boiled with the spaghetti. You feel yourself passing out. You don't know which is worse: drowning or boiling to death.

Then you wonder: Do you have any chance of surviving?

No pasta-bility!

THE END

34

Then you . . . wake up.

You sit up with a jolt. Your heart is pounding. The sheets and pillow are damp with sweat.

Could it be? you wonder. Was it all just a dream?

Your heart skips a beat as the door to your room opens. Who is going to come in? The Sleep Master? Space aliens? You get ready to run for your life.

Who does come into the room makes you almost faint. Your parents. Looking totally normal.

It really was just a dream — a terrible, wild dream.

"Mom! Dad!" you shout. "It's you!"

"Of course it's us, silly," your mom says with a smile. "Who did you think it was?"

"How was your night?" your dad asks later, downstairs at the breakfast table.

"Uh, not so great. But everything's okay now."

"Good," he replies. "Dear," he adds, turning to your mom, "could you please pass the bowl of zzortaxx and freeemin? I still can't get used to Earth food."

THE END

You jump — and slide through the gap with inches to spare. Behind you, the falling ceiling scrapes your feet.

CRUNCH! You hit the dirt outside and roll over.

The house is gone! There's just a hole in the ground. That dream house definitely wasn't the house of your dreams. It was a nightmare!

Shakily, you get up and dust yourself off. Are you still dreaming? You feel confused. You walk to the hole where the house once was. Are you hearing things, or are there voices calling out from deep inside the pit?

"Help! Get us out of here!"

It sounds like —

Your parents! They must have been in the house when it collapsed!

"Mom! Dad!" you yell. "Hold on! I'll get you out!" But how? You could try to crawl down the slanted side of the pit. Or you could try to get a light to see what's down there.

Which do you do?

If you climb down, go to PAGE 101.
If you look for a light, go to PAGE 113.

36

"Whoa!" you cry. You throw yourself backwards — out of reach of Mr. Bumber's hands.

Unfortunately, as you go down, you accidentally slam your head against the microphone. You're knocked cold.

Next thing you know, you're waking up in a hospital. You overhear a nurse saying, "Because of an accident, this poor patient has delusions of being a school principal."

But you *are* the principal, you think. You can't remember being anything else.

For the rest of your life, you tell anyone who'll listen, "I'm the principal, I'm the principal, I'm the principal. . . ."

THE END

Frantically, you try to dream up some way to escape. Nothing happens. No matter what you think of, you're still in the black hole.

"Even dreams can't escape from a black hole," you groan. What more could possibly go wrong?

This dream stuff really stinks!

Then your mother interrupts your thoughts. "Don't worry, dear," she tells you. "We're not alone. I don't know how it happened, but your teacher is here too. So you don't even have to miss a day of school! Isn't that terrific?"

THE END

Why should I be friends with those snobs? you think. Instead, you head toward the misfits. Besides, you tell yourself, I can help these guys become popular.

You walk down the steps to Benny, Alicia, and the rest of the school outcasts. They're grateful you came over.

"So, what do you want to do?" Benny asks. "Hang out?"

"How about going to the soccer game?" Alicia chimes in.

"Nah," Benny replies. "Sports are boring. Let's play video games!"

They all turn to you.

"Why don't you decide?" Alicia suggests.

If you go to the soccer game, turn to PAGE 135.
If you go play video games, turn to PAGE 25.

In a flash the two of you are standing at the back of a large auditorium. Thousands of people fill the seats. A banner over the stage reads:

THE GREAT DEBATE

On the stage are two stands for speakers. At one stand is a tall, dark figure dressed in black from head to foot. Even though the hall is brightly lit, you can't make out his face.

"That's Lord Morphos," the Sleep Master whispers. "He's waiting for you to debate him."

Suddenly, everyone in the hall turns to stare at you. It's so silent you hear your heart beating. The dark lord of dreams points at you and softly hisses your name.

You're frozen with fear. Do you dare debate him? All you really want to do is run like mad. What do you do?

If you go up to the stage, go to PAGE 41.

If you tear out of the auditorium, go to PAGE 80.

Of course you can fly. This is a dream, right?

I can do it, you think. I can fly. And right away you begin to rise up into the air. Soon the meadow and the lake are small shapes far below. You can't believe how easy it is.

"Wow!" you shout. "I'm flying! Yahoo!"

Your heart is beating quickly.

"This is great!" you cry, as you turn effortlessly, high above the earth. "I'm like a bird. Nah. More like — a bat!"

A moth flutters by a few feet away. You dive through the sky. Mouth open, you gulp it in midair.

Mmm, that was tasty, you think.

Then it hits you.

"Yuck!" you squeak. "I just ate a moth!"

Fly to PAGE 85.

You can't back out now. You take a deep breath and walk to the stage. You're so nervous you can barely put one foot in front of the other.

Now you're on the stage. It's your turn to speak.

You grab the microphone. You clear your throat. You open your mouth. There's only one problem.

You don't know what the debate is about. You haven't the faintest idea of what to say.

Notes! you think. I must have written notes.

You frantically reach for notes in your pants pocket. But you can't find them.

Because you're not wearing any pants!

You're standing on the stage in your underwear!

The audience erupts in laughter, jeering and guffawing. You've lost the debate without saying a word!

The Sleep Master appears next to you. "You lost, you dope!" he yells. "Now you're trapped here forever in your underwear!"

Talk about being caught with your pants down!

THE END

"Who says we're not real?"

Your eyes pop open. Who said that?

NO! IMPOSSIBLE!

A gargoyle is winking at you!

"AHHHHH!" you scream. You pull the sheets over your head.

But after a few seconds, you have to take a peek.

Four strange creatures are flitting around the room. They hop from the headboard to the dresser to the lamp, playing tag and turning somersaults in the air. Each one is about a foot tall, with leathery wings. There's a gorilla, a serpent-headed dog, a devil, and a man with no eyes.

You want to speak. But there's a lump in your throat the size of a softball. Finally, words spill out.

"Wha — wha —" you stammer. Well, words *almost* spill out.

"What are we doing here?" the dog finishes for you. "We're in your dream, dummy!"

So that's it! You finally fell asleep. "Okay, fine, no problemo," you tell the gargoyles. "I'll wake myself up."

"Wait!" the gorilla says quickly. "Don't wake up yet. We haven't told you the secret of the bed!"

Learn more on PAGE 29.

And find yourself frozen in one spot, unable to move.

"Hey!" you moan through a stiff mouth. "I can't move."

"Stop complaining," a nearby voice responds. "Wait till you've been standing over this bed for twelve hours."

Bed?

You can't move your head. But you can see that you're back in the room at the inn. Above the bed.

NO! You're part of the headboard!

Somehow you've become a gargoyle!

"Hey! No fair!" you screech. "I didn't dream this!"

"True," the devil gargoyle replies. "But you did volunteer. We appreciate it. We all need some time off."

"I didn't volunteer," you claim. Then you remember your words to the dog gargoyle: *If there's anything I can do for you . . .*

The devil smirks. "You're going to take our places, one at a time. Ten years for each of us."

You strain to break free, but you're stuck like glue.

"The forty years will go by quickly," the gorilla promises. "And don't forget: Once a week they polish us."

Well, at least you'll have your moment to shine!

THE END

You run until your four legs are burning with pain. But you can't escape the nightmare animals. You gasp for breath.

And then you race over to a tableful of water bottles. You grab one with your hand and pour it over your head.

Hand?

With a surge of joy you realize you're human again. The horse-monsters have vanished. Instead of a grassy hillside, you're jogging along a city street. On all sides are hundreds of other runners.

Check it out! You're in the New York City Marathon!

And boy, are you out of breath! You've got to stop running!

"Come on!" a voice pleads. "Don't quit now!"

You glance to your right.

Eek! It's the Sleep Master!

Hear what he has to say on PAGE 115.

Suddenly you can't breathe.

But it's not because of shock. It's because something is covering up your mouth and nose!

What happened? You were just in the Buddy Burger. Now you're in the dark — and something is choking you!

You reach up to your face and clutch at whatever it is, fighting for your life. Fiercely, you tear away the —

Pile of money!

What? You stare around you in confusion.

You're in bed. Back at the inn. The dream is over.

Sort of.

You're surrounded by a pile of money! You grab a stack of hundred-dollar bills.

There must be a million dollars here. Just as Buddy said!

"Yahoo!" you scream and start jumping up and down on the bed. The noise brings your parents running in.

"What's going on here?" your father asks, rubbing the sleep out of his eyes.

"Hey, Dad!" You laugh uncontrollably. "This vacation has definitely been a rewarding experience!"

THE END

The last thing you need is to be more scared. You put down the GOOSEBUMPS book and take a look at *Dr. Morphos's Sleep Remedies.*

You turn on a lamp and sit back in a large easy chair. You open the dusty leather book. You read the first page.

CAN'T SLEEP? it says in large block letters.

Genius guess, you think. You read on.

You can see right away the book is bogus. All its sleep remedies were invented back in 1903.

Still, they might be good for a laugh.

You feel a big yawn coming on. Gee, you think, this is working already. I can barely keep my eyes open.

Turn to PAGE 79.

"I'm outta here!" you scream.

You race to the door. Except there's no door!

"Dirt in motion!" the vaporizer announces. You hear it wheel toward you. You see it raise its laser cannon.

"Targeting procedure commencing!" it announces.

"Where is that door?" you shout in frustration.

Suddenly, the outline of the door appears.

"Hello!" the door says. "Leaving so soon?"

At the same time you hear the vaporizer say, "Target dirt locked in. Fire in five seconds. Five . . . four . . ."

"Open up!" you order the door.

"Of course," it purrs. "Did you remember your coat?"

"I wasn't wearing a coat!" you scream.

"Oh, dear," the door murmurs. "My memory banks need an overhaul."

"Three . . . two . . ."

"Want to hear the weather report?" the door asks.

"One!" announces the vaporizer.

You brace yourself for the burst of laser fire. Just before it hits, you hear the door exclaim, "Have a nice day!"

THE END

No way you're sharing the glory with teammates.

You shoot! The goalie dives for it . . .

And misses!

The ball bounces in. You scored the goal!

The crowd goes berserk.

Your teammates are going berserk. And the opposing team is laughing and slapping you on the back. "Way to go, dork!" they laugh.

Your face turns red when you discover why.

You scored a goal against your own team! That's why the goalie was waving. And why your teammate wanted the ball.

The game ends. Your team loses by one goal.

"You lost us the championship," roars your coach. "And now you're going to pay the price. Get him, guys!"

Your teammates start chasing you around the stadium. "It's just a game," you cry out. Pointlessly.

When they catch up to you, they throw you to the ground. Their shoes come down on you again and again.

As you lose consciousness, you hear Benny sneer, "Hey, loser! I guess you really *do* get a kick out of soccer."

THE END

You're in Marky World, home of Marky Mouse! That's not a real castle. It's part of a stupid theme park for little kids!

The shadowy figure isn't a knight. It's a five-foot-tall mouse wearing a bow tie and white gloves! Marky Mouse!

"I can't believe it!" you moan in disappointment.

Your mom and dad stroll up beside you. They're dressed in shorts and T-shirts. Your dad has a big camera slung around his neck.

"Oh, look!" he cries. "It's Marky Mouse. Go stand next to him. I'll take your picture!"

"Oh, that'll be so *cute*," your mom gushes.

"Dad! Mom! Please!" you groan. You are so embarrassed.

Marky Mouse steps up and drapes his arm around your shoulder. You squirm miserably.

"Smile!" your dad chirps.

"I have the day all planned," your mother declares. "First, we'll ride the spinning teakettle, then we'll see the 3-D film on how plastic is made, then we'll visit the singing animatronic parakeets, and then . . ."

Oh, man. This nightmare is just beginning!

THE END

No, cheating is wrong, you tell yourself. Besides, you might get caught.

You find yourself seated at an empty desk. The teacher at the front of the room announces, "Please turn over your paper and begin. You have fifteen seconds."

Fifteen seconds! For the whole test? Nervously, you turn the paper over and look at it.

It says:

THE MOST IMPORTANT TEST IN YOUR LIFE
Please circle the correct answer.
Why did the chicken cross the road?
a) To get to the other side.
b) $E=MC^2$

You can't believe it! This is the most important test of your life?

The answer is obvious.

Or is this a trick question?

You glance at the clock. There are only four seconds left. You have to choose. What's the answer?

If you pick answer A, go to PAGE 126.
If you pick answer B, go to PAGE 117.

The Sleep Master points ahead. You see an opposing army lined up to meet you. Wow! It's even larger than your own!

In the center of the enemy force is a tall figure on a black stallion. His black shield has white *Z*'s painted on it.

Across the distance separating the two armies, his black eyes find you. He nods, as if daring you to attack. The fear in the pit of your stomach tells you the knight is Lord Morphos.

"We await your orders," the Sleep Master utters. "Shall we attack? Or do you wish to meet Lord Morphos in single combat?"

"Uh — I —" you stutter.

The anger you felt a moment ago is turning into anxiety. What did you get yourself into? You can't lead an army. And you sure don't want to fight that maniac by yourself.

Everyone's watching you, waiting for a signal.

What'll it be, hotshot general?

If you lead a charge, go to PAGE 7.

If you challenge Lord Morphos to single combat, go to PAGE 89.

"Get to work!" a deep voice booms at you.

"Yeah, yeah," you grumble.

The computer's central processing unit is bugging you again. That's the third time in the last tenth of a second. All because some stupid kid wants to play computer chess again.

"Get to work!" the voice says again.

"All right!" you groan.

You remember when *you* were a kid. It seems like centuries ago — but then, human time is so slow compared to computer time.

You wait while the kid decides on his first move. It may only be a minute to him, but to you it feels like three weeks. There's nothing to do but sit and count the nanoseconds.

You're so bored, you decide to crash the program for kicks.

"Hah!" you sneer as the pieces freeze on the screen. "How do you like *that* play, you little brat?"

Talk about having a silicon chip on your shoulder!

THE END

Hmmm. Maybe watching the tube will make you fall asleep. You pick up the remote control and turn on the TV.

The show you're watching must be some kind of documentary. There's only one character. And all the person does is sleep.

"Boring!" you grumble and change the channel.

The same program is on the new channel. You keep hitting the remote control button. But every channel shows a person asleep in a bed.

"What is this?" you ask aloud. "Sleep TV?"

Just then, the actor in the show rolls over. You gasp.

It's you!

In your dream, you're watching yourself sleep back at the inn! Then you notice a time display in the lower right corner. Hey. The picture you're watching is on videotape!

What would happen if you fast-forwarded? Would you see the future? Or what if you hit the rewind button? Could you see the past?

Your hand hovers over the remote control.

If you rewind, go to PAGE 109.
If you fast-forward, go to PAGE 10.

54

You turn to the page marked "Wonderful Dream World."

At first, the instructions make you laugh.

1. THINK WONDERFUL, BEAUTIFUL THOUGHTS. SOON YOU'LL BE HAVING WONDERFUL, BEAUTIFUL DREAMS.

"Yeah, right," you mutter. You read on.

2. COUNT BACKWARDS BY SEVENS, STARTING WITH 539.

3. ALSO, IMAGINE SEA SQUIDS JUMPING OVER A FENCE.

4. ON EVERY THIRD NUMBER, HUM "YANKEE DOODLE."

Huh? How can you fall asleep doing all of that? You giggle as you start counting.

"539, 532, 525, 518 . . . This will never work," you mumble. "It's ridicul —"

Yawn.

Your eyelids feel heavy.

"455, 448, 441, 434 . . ."

You feel yourself slipping away.

Slip to PAGE 87.

Your house is gone. It's been replaced by a home that looks like a combination spaceship and video game machine. It's all covered with flashing neon lights.

"Excellent," you murmur, and step up to the door.

"Hello!" the door says in a pleasant robotic voice. "I am now reading your DNA profile. Thank you. Welcome home!"

The door vanishes. You step through an open space. Inside, the house is even more fantastic. The walls glow with colored patterns. The furniture moves and talks. A couch comes up to you.

"Would you like to sit?" it asks. You plop yourself down.

A hologram of a butler appears next to you. He's a tall, distinguished-looking man dressed in a tuxedo.

"Good day," the hologram says. "What would you like to do today? I could arrange an Extreme Party. Or, if you prefer, I could have the computer do your chores."

A party would be fun. But it would also be great to have someone else do your chores. Which will it be?

If you say "do my chores," go to PAGE 110.
If you ask for a party, go to PAGE 127.

It's really not a hard decision.

"I want to go home," you say.

The Sleep Master nods his head. And suddenly — you're back in the chair at the inn, exactly where you fell asleep. You did it! You can hardly wait to get upstairs and see your parents.

You start to jump up out of the chair.

YIKES!

You're floating above the chair. And you're wearing a space suit. In front of you is a giant view-screen filled with millions of stars.

More shocking is the sight of your mother and father sitting on either side. They're also dressed like astronauts!

"Mom? Dad?" you blurt out. "What's happening?"

"We're going into warp five," your mother replies calmly.

"But . . . but . . . we're in a spaceship!"

"Of course we are," she replies. "This is where we live."

"No —" you begin, but a familiar voice interrupts you.

"It is *now*," says the Sleep Master.

Take hyperdrive to PAGE 73.

You find yourself in bed, at the inn. It's morning. Daylight is streaming through the windows. You stretch against the warm, soft mattress and let out a happy sigh.

What a weird dream, you think, feeling relaxed. I bet that's the last I'll ever see of the Sleep Master.

You realize you're starving. "Time for breakfast," you murmur and throw off the covers.

Then your heart stops beating. For the first time, you notice your skin. It's smooth. And green. Your fingers are webbed. And . . .

Turn to PAGE 8.

You take a deep breath and declare, “Sell!”

The next thing you know, the table, the executives, and the room are all gone!

“Sell!” someone is yelling at you. “Sell those burgers!”

You’re feeling mixed up. The noise, the smells, the crowds of people — where are you?

When you see your orange uniform, you know.

You’re working in a fast-food restaurant!

The tubby woman snarling at you is the manager. “I said sell those burgers!” she repeats gruffly. “And remember, the customer is always right!”

“Uh, yes, ma’am,” you mumble. This dream is weird! But who knows? It could be fun, you think.

You turn to greet the customers. “Welcome to Buddy Burgers!” you tell the first person in line.

“Uh, like, uh, yeah,” the teenager says. “Give me, like, uh, like a Buddy Special Burger, well done, with extra pickles, and like, no like, cheese, no onion, mayonnaise, hold the mustard, and a side order of, like, fries.”

Order up on PAGE 30.

"I'm home!" you cry.

It's true. You're back at your own house. You're standing at your own front door. No more weird inns, no more freaky gargoyles.

Wait a minute! The gargoyles!

You're not really home. You're *dreaming* you're home! You put your hand on the doorknob. Then you stop.

"Hey, whatever I dream will come true!" you say to yourself. "That means I could dream up something right now. Something that will make being home *really* cool."

You could make it into a high-tech entertainment center. You're thinking built-in movie theater, swimming pool — plus all the other stuff your parents would never let you have.

You get an even better idea. What if you dreamed of a home where *you* were the boss, where you got to tell your parents what to do for once? Now that would be really cool.

You stand there, deciding what to dream.

If you dream of a new house, go to PAGE 55.
If you dream you're the boss, go to PAGE 62.

The laser beam strikes the spot you just stood on.

This dream stinks!

Then, suddenly, you get an idea. You know how to find the central computer.

"Computer!" you order. "Where are you?"

A panel in a wall opens. Out pops a small black box.

"Here I am!" says the box.

With a flood of relief, you grab it. The box will turn off the vaporizer. But when you glance at it, you feel sick. The box has no screen, no keyboard.

It only has two blue buttons. One is marked ON/OFF. The other is marked ALARM.

The vaporizer is right behind you. Spinning around, you see the laser aimed straight at you. You have to press one of the buttons — fast! Which will it be?

If you press ALARM, *go to PAGE 134.*
If you press ON/OFF, *go to PAGE 121.*

Forget about him, you think. You just want to go home. One thing the Sleep Master said made sense. You entered this crazy dream by falling asleep in your world. So maybe the way out is to fall asleep in this world.

Okay. I'll sack out, you decide. You lie down on the soft grass.

And find yourself sinking into stinking brown mud! The entire field has changed into an oozy sinkhole!

You twist and turn, trying to stand up. But the mud just sucks you deeper.

"Help!" you scream. But there's no one around. Now the ghastly crud is up to your mouth. You start to gag.

"It's only a dream!" you cry.

But this sinking feeling is for real. You're actually being buried alive — and the worst part is, you keep hearing the words to that stupid nursery rhyme:

Row, row, row your boat, gently down the stream,

Merrily, merrily, merrily, merrily,

Life is but a —

SCHLURP!

THE END

You open the door and shout, "Mom, Dad, I'm home!" Your parents come running downstairs and stand at attention in the hallway.

"Welcome home," your dad says. "What can I do for you? Massage your feet? Bring you some comic books?"

You can hardly reply at first. You're in shock. This dream is already better than you could have, well, dreamed.

"How about cleaning my room?" you ask.

"Yes!" your dad declares. "I'd be very happy to!"

"And make my allowance a thousand dollars a week!"

"Done!" your dad cries, running to clean your room.

"Your favorite snacks are waiting in the living room," your mom announces. She curtsies to you. "And after you eat, you can watch three hours of TV while I do your homework."

You throw yourself down on the couch.

"This is fantastic!" you cry. "They're like robots!"

You put your feet on the coffee table. Hey, that's funny. Your legs feel kind of stiff.

You glance at your feet.

Yikes! They're turning to polished steel!

Steel yourself for what's on PAGE 18.

As you try to decide, you glance at the headboard.

Hey! Did one of the gargoyles just wink at you?

"That's it!" you bark. "I'm out of here!"

Your feet slide over the cold wooden floor. You tiptoe down the stairs. At the bottom you switch on a light and see . . .

No monsters. Whew! So far, so good.

You nervously head for the kitchen. On the way, you pass through the old-fashioned sitting room. You notice a tall bookcase, crammed with old yellowing volumes. Maybe a book will calm you down.

You glance at the titles. One old book catches your eye. You pull it out. You have to blow the dust away to read the title:

"*Dr. Morphos's Sleep Remedies,*" you read aloud. How corny can you get? you think. Then you spot a worn paperback on a lower shelf. You recognize it right away. It's one of your favorites — a book in the GOOSEBUMPS series. The cover says *Give Yourself GOOSEBUMPS #456: Nightmares Are No Fun.*

It looks really scary. But it could be fun.

Which book do you choose?

If you read Dr. Morphos's Sleep Remedies, *go to PAGE 46.*

If you read the GOOSEBUMPS book, go to PAGE 128.

You're about to incinerate the Sleep Master.

But you stop.

Maybe it's the look on his face. Or maybe it's that you've finally got the upper hand on him. Whatever it is, you decide to listen to him.

Instantly, you're not a dragon anymore. You're back in human form, sitting by the lake. The Sleep Master sits across from you. He looks like a teenage boy.

"It's a good thing you chose to listen," he says. "You think you're dreaming now? No way. This is reality, friend. Everything you thought was real — your parents, your home, your school, your life — *that's* the dream."

"Give me a break." You laugh. "This can't be real. I was just flying around like a dragon."

"Yeah," he answers. "But in the real world, this world, crazy stuff happens all the time."

The kid continues. "The deal is, you've been asleep now for a long, long time. I've been trying to wake you up. I finally did it. Congratulations! You're awake."

Rise and shine on PAGE 70.

Your finger starts to press the EJECT button. Until you realize something: You're not wearing a parachute!

KABLAMMMMM!

Your jet is exploding from the Sleep Master's rocket. But somehow, you're alive.

You flap your huge wings and twist your spiked tail. Now you're in the path of the Sleep Master's jet. He looks annoyed.

A moment later, he's really hot under the collar. That's because you spit a ball of flame at his on-coming fighter.

Hot stuff! you think. I'm a fire-breathing dragon! The Sleep Master's jet twists aside. But you chase it. You're right behind it. One fireball from you and he'll be ashes. You feel flames building up inside your chest.

But before you let them fly, the Sleep Master calls out to you.

"Don't do it!" he shouts. "You're not dreaming! This is real! You have to let me explain!"

If you listen to the Sleep Master, go to PAGE 64.
If you breathe fire on him, go to PAGE 131.

The more you think about Morphos, the angrier you get. Ever since you started this dream, you've been pushed around. Now you're ready to fight back.

"I choose battle!" you shout. "Let's rumble!"

The Sleep Master smiles grimly and nods. In a flash you find yourself dressed in shining armor, a lance in your hand. You're sitting astride a mighty charger.

The Sleep Master perches on a horse next to you. The two of you are in the middle of a vast field.

The Sleep Master holds a long red pennant in one hand and a golden trumpet in the other. As you watch in awe, he blows a single note on the trumpet.

Instantly the field around you is filled with a mighty army. There are hundreds of soldiers in chain mail, knights on horseback, and archers.

"This is your army," the Sleep Master shouts over the din. "Now lead us!"

March to PAGE 51.

The chessboard vanishes. You're sitting in front of a small computer screen. A man's face gazes at you.

"Congratulations!" he says with a smile. "You've just beaten our champion chess program. As a reward, we're going to turn *you* into a computer program!"

You suddenly find yourself in darkness. You hear a whirring sound. Whoa! You're in the computer! You've been turned into a computer chess program!

See what it's like on PAGE 52.

RING!

It's the late bell. You're standing in front of your school, books in hand.

"Rats," you mutter. "I'm late for class."

Then it hits you.

This is a dream. A very real-seeming dream.

And you're in total control of what happens.

A surge of excitement pulses through you. "Thank you, gargoyles!" you cry. "This is going to be so awesome."

You hurry through the front doors. Then an angry voice stops you dead in your tracks.

"You there!" A bald, chunky teacher marches up to you. Mr. LaGamba. He points his finger at you.

"You! Report to the principal's office!"

For a moment your heart sinks. But then you think: Who is he kidding? This is *my* dream, isn't it?

Then again, it could be fun to mess with the principal now that you're in charge. What do you do?

If you go to the principal, go to PAGE 114.
If you don't, go to PAGE 120.

The Sleep Master is the key to getting home. You're sure of it.

You gallop over the grass in the direction you last saw him heading. You fly over the next hill — and the next.

In the distance you see the ocean. And something else. Something you can't believe you're seeing.

It's the inn where you and your parents are staying!

That's where you fell asleep and started having this crazy dream. And now the inn is *in* your dream.

Can things get any screwier?

You turn toward the old inn. You trot up to the porch. NO HORSES ALLOWED INSIDE reads a sign on the door.

Darn! But wait. You peer down at your hooves.

They're feet! You're human again!

You push open the door and run inside.

"Mom! Dad! I'm back," you shout.

But there's no answer.

Where is everybody?

Find out on PAGE 20.

"This can't be the real world," you protest.

"How do you know what's a dream and what's real?" the Sleep Master asks.

"But *this* is the dream!" you shout. You feel confused and scared. Could the Sleep Master be telling the truth? Is everything you've always believed in really a dream?

You jump up. "I don't care what's real!" you cry. "I want to go home!"

"Sorry." The Sleep Master shrugs. "No can do. Enjoy your new life."

"But . . ." you begin.

Too late. The Sleep Master has turned into a black stallion. He gallops away across the field.

"Stop!" you scream. You start to chase him. You want the Sleep Master to explain more.

Then you stop and think. There may be a way out of here. If you fall asleep, you might wake up back in your own reality.

Which do you choose?

If you chase the Sleep Master, go to PAGE 102.

If you lie down and try to sleep, go to PAGE 61.

"Use my noodle," you repeat. "Right. I have to think harder."

You concentrate with all your might. But your brain isn't up to the job. You feel just a wee bit too dumb.

"Yeow!" you shout. A blinding pain shoots through your head. In the reflection of the glass tank you see what caused it. Your head is growing! And so is your brain.

The pain stops. But your head keeps expanding until it's the size of a basketball. Then a beach ball. You're feeling much smarter. The answer to the riddle is as plain as day.

TICK . . . TICK . . . BONG!

"Your time is up," rumbles Lord Morphos.

"That's okay," you reply. "I know the answer. The answer is: *There aren't any orangutans in Brazil!*"

"That's correct," hisses Morphos. "How did you do it?"

Silence falls over the room. Sweat drips from your huge head. Your life hinges on getting this correct!

"I used my noodle," you reply proudly.

Go to PAGE 124.

Your father slides out of bed. He towers over you on two long, spindly legs. His eight-fingered hands reach out.

"Time to go hooome," he whispers in an eerie voice.

"H-h-home?" you stammer. You can barely speak.

The eight-foot-tall creature who was your mother shuffles toward you. She points up, toward the ceiling.

"Hooome," she repeats. And then they both grab you.

Their fingers are cold and strong. Their blood-red eyes stare at you. You are limp with fear.

"Mom! Dad!" you scream. "Let me go!"

But your screams are drowned out by a loud humming noise. Bright lights fill the sky. The aliens drag you to the window. You see a space-ship landing next to the inn.

"Do not be scaaared," your mom whispers. "Our experiments do not hurt . . . much."

"Yesss," your dad murmurs. "We need new subjects."

"No!" you shout. "Let me go!" Then you . . .

Turn to PAGE 34.

You can't believe your eyes. The Sleep Master is also decked out in a space suit.

"You liar!" you shout. "You said I could go back to reality."

"But you have," he explains. "I said if you defeated Lord Morphos, I'd also return. I guess I brought my powers with me. I can change things here, like I did in my reality. This is my new dream world!"

"Stop this!" you command the Sleep Master. "I want you to make everything normal, right now!"

"Sorry," he replies. "From now on, this *is* normal."

"Strap yourselves in!" shouts your mom. "When we're out of hyperdrive, I'll serve lunch."

Traveling through space with your parents? You're about to scream in protest, but then it hits you.

This could be the greatest road trip ever!

"What do you say?" asks the Sleep Master. "You want to give it a try?"

"Sure," you reply with a big grin. "But I get the window seat!"

THE END

Then it hits you. This screwy dream world! It keeps changing everything around on you!

"The lake," you gasp. "It's a mirage!"

You drop to the sand, the sun broiling the back of your neck. In a few moments you'll be burned to a crisp.

Looks like your goose is really cooked this time.

THE END

It's no use. You can't go any farther. Besides, you decide, you shouldn't trust the Sleep Master.

Suddenly, a couch appears in front of you. Right in the middle of the street. Then the marathon disappears.

You're used to weird changes by now. So what comes next doesn't even make you blink.

You find yourself lying on the couch in a fancy doctor's office. Across from you sits a small man wearing a tweed suit. In his hand is a pad. He's writing busily.

"I'm your psychoanalyst," he explains. "Describe your dreams, please."

"I thought *this* was a dream!" you sputter.

"Ah, you're suffering from a terrible disease," he answers. "You have a displaced subconscious preverbal fixation with adenoidal tendencies."

"I do?" you ask in dismay. "What's that?"

"You're all mixed up. Luckily, I know the cure. Just say the opposite of what I say."

Is it possible? Could this doctor really cure you?

Do you do what the psychoanalyst says? If so, go to PAGE 6.

If you refuse, go to PAGE 92.

"Wake up, come on, wake up!"

Someone is shaking you awake. It's your mom! She's standing over your bed at the inn and shaking your shoulder.

"Come on, wake up, sleepyhead," she repeats. "I have some very important news!"

You sit up. That was some dream! It seemed so real.

"The strangest thing just happened," your mom gushes. "Your principal called us. He said you did an amazing job on your last test."

"What?" Your heart is pounding. Could it be?

"Yes," your mom continues with a grin. "In fact, you scored so well, he said you never have to go to school again!"

You glance at the headboard. Did one of the gargoyles just wink at you?

"Well," your mom asks, "aren't you going to say something?"

"Yeah," you reply. "Could we buy this headboard and take it home?"

THE END

"Extra cheese!" you call out, hoping you got it right. Seconds later, a steaming hot Buddy Burger comes sliding down a chute. You hand it to the teenager.

He lifts one corner of the paper wrapper and stares at the Buddy Burger.

"Hey!" he exclaims. "This has, like, extra cheese! I didn't, like, order any cheese!"

Uh-oh. "I'm sorry, sir!" You reach for the burger. "I'll get you a new one right away."

"No way!" The teenager snatches the burger from you. "No one has ever given me extra cheese before! I'm going to give you a tip!"

He snaps his fingers. A tall, distinguished-looking man in a blue suit steps up to the counter.

"Roberts!" the teenager says. "Give this wonderful kid a tip. Make it a million!"

"A million?" you repeat, trying to catch your breath.

"Sure," the teenager says. "Don't you know who I am? I own Buddy Burgers. I'm Buddy!"

Roberts lifts a black leather case onto the counter and turns it over. Out pour stacks of hundred-dollar bills!

Go to PAGE 45.

"Hold the mustard!" you say into the microphone.

"Hold the mustard!" the cook shouts back.

"Hold the mustard!" the manager yells.

You notice the customers staring up above your head. You also glance up. And nearly have a heart attack.

A ten-foot-tall plastic mustard bottle is falling on you!

When the bottle hits, it pins you to the floor like Hulk Hogan. You can't move. You can barely breathe.

But you're in luck. The manager has arrived. You wait for her to lift off the bottle.

Instead she glares down at you and screams, "I said HOLD the mustard! Are you holding the mustard? Or is the mustard holding you?"

The teenage customer peers at you over the counter.

"Hey, I ordered fries," he demands. "Where are they?"

You're about to tell him to get lost, but then you remember what the manager said — the customer is always right. What do you do?

If you tell him off, go to PAGE 107.
If you try to get his fries, go to PAGE 86.

You turn the page.

At the top of this page is a warning in boldface letters.

ADVANCED SELF-HYPNOSIS METHOD. USE WITH EXTREME CAUTION!

There are two listings here. The first is "Beautiful Dreamer: Guaranteed to give you the deepest, most restful sleep you've ever had."

The second is "Wonderful Dream World: Fill your night with lovely dreams."

Hmmm. Maybe I should try one of these, you think. But which one?

If you choose "Beautiful Dreamer," go to PAGE 24.

If you choose "Wonderful Dream World," go to PAGE 54.

How can I debate Lord Morphos? you think. I'm not prepared. I don't even know what the debate is about.

"Sorry," you say to the Sleep Master. "I just got a real bad case of stage fright."

You whirl around and dash out of the room.

You find yourself in another room. You let out a gasp and come to a screeching halt. In front of you is a huge tank filled with clear liquid. But that's not what scares you.

Floating in the tank is a human brain the size of a car. A *big* car.

You hear a deep voice coming from somewhere in the tank. Then you realize the voice is actually inside your head. You're hearing the thoughts of the giant brain.

"I am Lord Morphos," it announces. "You have challenged me to a test of wits. I have taken the form that gives my brain the most power. Are you ready for the contest?"

You're not. But you have a feeling you don't have any choice. You grit your teeth. Might as well get it over with.

"Okay," you say grimly. "Let's get thinking!"

Go to PAGE 27.

Your teammate has a better shot, so you pass the ball. Your teammate shoots and scores.

GOOOOOOOOOOOOOOOOAL!

Your team eventually wins by one goal. The crowd goes nuts. Spectators rush out onto the field. You're a hero!

The soccer coach forces his way through the crowd. The coach shouts, "I just got a call from the U.S. pro soccer league. They want you in the World Cup!"

You're so happy, you decide to play for the fun of it. For free.

This is the greatest moment of your life. You only wish you could tell your folks about it. . . .

"Wake up! Come on, sleepyhead. Rise and shine!"

You open your eyes. You're back in bed at the inn. Your mom is waking you up.

You recall your dream with a chill. Play soccer for free? No shoe contract? No TV commercials? Are you kidding?

Next time, you'd better dream you have a sports agent!

THE END

"Uh, no, thanks," you reply. You don't trust the gargoyles! Thanks to them your house and your parents have disappeared down a black hole.

The dog gargoyle shrugs and flaps away. "It's your funeral," it calls over its shoulder.

You shudder. You wish it hadn't put it like that.

You turn your attention back to the oil lamp. How can you light it? In desperation, you reach into your pockets, hoping to find something you can use.

Amazingly, your hand closes around a box of matches!

"Who needs gargoyles?" you sneer.

You take a match out of the box and light it.

Funny. You never noticed that giant pile of dynamite you were sitting on. Not until you lit the match.

But look on the bright side. You wanted this dream to be a blast!

THE END

The Sleep Master roars past you in a sleek blue-and-silver jet fighter. He waves at you. Then his plane banks hard. He's behind you again!

KACK-KACK-KACK-KACK!

Another burst of bullets sprays across your wing. The Sleep Master is right on your tail! His gun is locked on you.

Your heart is in your mouth. "I'm finished," you moan.

Then your eyes land on a red button marked EJECT. It's your only chance for escape!

But what if you're over the middle of the ocean?

Do you push it?

If you push the eject button, go to PAGE 5.
If you don't push it, go to PAGE 65.

Something tells you that you really should pick up that mouse.

As you lift it, the mouse changes. It's no longer soft, round, and furry. It's hard, square, and made of plastic.

This is a *computer* mouse! you realize.

You also notice that the knight has stopped dead in his tracks. He's motionless.

Aha! "The mouse controls the game!" you shout.

A robotlike voice echoes above the chessboard. It's the voice of the computer.

"Your move," the computer tells you.

You study the board. Oh, man. You have no idea what to do.

Feeling rattled, you think, I can't let a computer beat me.

Nervously, you move the computer mouse. A white pawn jumps ahead one space.

"Checkmate! You win!" the computer declares.

"I do?" you gasp in disbelief. "What do I win?"

Jump to PAGE 67.

In shock, you put your hands to your mouth.

Just as quickly, you jerk them away. You're covered with hairy, leathery skin! You have claws and webbed fingers. Yecch!

You really have turned into a bat!

Despite your horror, instinct takes over. You flap your wings. You bounce high-pitched sound waves off objects. And it all seems as natural as riding a bike.

For some reason, you get an urge to fly toward a nearby hill. Gliding closer, you see the dark mouth of a giant cave. Whoa! The stench of bat droppings fills your sensitive nostrils.

The human part of you wants to turn back. But the bat part of you is happy to be home.

Guess which part wins.

You fly into the darkness. Then you expertly flit upside down. The claws on your feet grab the cave ceiling. You know you're only dreaming. But then you remember something. *Hey! I was supposed to have wonderful dreams!*

"It *is* wonderful, if you're a bat," says a familiar voice.

Find out whose voice it is on PAGE 96.

The customer is always right, you remind yourself.

With a tremendous effort, you heave the giant mustard bottle off your back. Oooh, your ribs are killing you!

You limp to the fries bin. Got to get those fries!

Hmmm. The bin is empty.

"Okay. Not a problem," you mutter. You can handle this! You stagger to the rear of the kitchen. That's where the electric fryer sits. The huge vat bubbles with hot oil.

You grab a twenty-pound sack of frozen french fries and carry it to the fryer. But some of the oil must have spilled on the floor. Because just as you hoist the bag over the boiling-hot oil, you slip.

There's nothing to grab hold of. You're tumbling headfirst into the fryer! You're going to be boiled to death!

"No!" you scream.

Slide over to PAGE 95.

The chair feels so soft, you could lie there forever.

Except the chair is tickling your back.

Then you realize you're lying in a green meadow.

The spooky inn by the sea is gone. Instead you're in a beautiful valley. At the bottom of the valley is a small lake.

I must be dreaming, you realize. Hey, this is a nice dream.

The sky looks so beautiful. It would be great to fly up there. And suddenly you know you *can* fly. All you have to do is try.

But the lake also looks wonderful — cool and refreshing. Maybe you'd rather go for a swim.

If you try to fly, go to PAGE 40.
If you go for a swim, turn to PAGE 90.

"What a crummy sword!" you shout in dismay.

"Of course," Lord Morphos laughs. "It's made of chocolate."

Lord Morphos trots over on his stallion and raises his sword over your neck.

"You've lost," he snarls. "Prepare to meet *thy* doom."

You've got to buy some time! You break off a piece of your sweet sword and offer him a piece.

"Bite?" you ask meekly.

Unfortunately, Morphos isn't a chocoholic.

He's a chopoholic!

THE END

"No," you declare with determination. "This is my fight."

Without another word, you spur your horse forward. At the top of your lungs you scream a challenge.

"Lord Morphos! This is between you and me!"

The leader of the opposing army gallops to meet you. Between the two armies, the two of you stop.

Lord Morphos laughs with contempt. "Choose your weapon!" he orders in a deep, gravelly voice.

Weapon? You hadn't thought of that. You glance down and see that you're carrying two weapons: a long broadsword and a short, sharp dagger.

As you make up your mind, the Sleep Master appears on his horse, next to you.

"Don't worry about it," he tells you. "Lord Morphos is just a big bag of wind." Then he vanishes.

A bag of wind? He looks pretty tough, you think.

It's time to fight. Which weapon do you choose?

If you choose the sword, go to PAGE 12.
If you choose the knife, go to PAGE 108.

The water is too inviting to pass up. You sprint down to the lake. There's a wide sand beach around it. As you run onto the sand, you can't wait to dive into the cool, clear water. You run toward it.

Funny, you didn't notice how hot it was before.

The hot sand is toasting the soles of your feet. Good thing the cool lake isn't far off.

You stagger toward it. Your legs begin to ache. But the lake is no closer than it was.

"Got to get off this beach," you mutter. You turn around to head back to the grass.

It's gone!

There's nothing but white sand as far as the eye can see.

You're trapped in the middle of a desert!

Huh? How can this be?

Think it out on PAGE 74.

You march through the door with your name on it.

The desk inside has a nameplate. Your name is on it.

You really are the principal!

Fantastic! you think. You have some great ideas for running the school. You announce them over the PA system: "My first order of the day is, I want students and teachers to bow to me at all times. Homework is optional. And there's no school on Mondays and Fridays."

Being principal rocks!

Just then, an irate teacher rushes in. It's Mr. Bumber, the shop teacher. "Have you gone crazy?" he roars.

"How dare you speak to me without bowing?" you demand.

"Why, you —" Mr. Bumber bellows. His face turns purple with rage.

Then he lunges across your desk and leaps for your throat!

Leap back on PAGE 36.

This is a *dream*, you remind yourself. I'm not going to trust this psychoanalyst. He's probably *crazy*!

"Aren't you going to follow my instructions?" the small man demands.

"Sorry, Doc," you reply.

"That's proof you need my help!" he insists. "Now say —" He suddenly breaks off and looks at his watch. "Time's up!" he cries. Then he jumps up and runs out of the room.

"So much for professional help," you mutter. "He was pretty kooky, anyway. I'll have to help myself."

You glance around the office. A telephone sits on the psychoanalyst's desk. Against the wall is a large television.

Which one is more likely to help you escape from this dream world?

If you turn on the TV, go to PAGE 53.

If you pick up the phone, go to PAGE 105.

You wake up back in the chair at the inn. In your hand is *Dr. Morphos's Sleep Remedies.*

"No! I don't want to wake up!" you cry. "Not now! I had it all! I was president! I had ten billion dollars! I was on MTV!"

There's only one thing you can do — fall back to sleep. Get back into that dream.

So you take another nap. And when you wake up, you *are* the president.

President of the Rip Van Winkle Club!

THE END

A battle is too chancy. Lord Morphos is able to change anything in this world. So he'd have no problem kicking your rear end. But in a battle of wits, he can't change what you think.

Can he?

You swallow hard. "A contest of wits," you declare.

The Sleep Master nods and waves a hand.

See what happens on PAGE 39.

"No!" you scream again — and jerk your head off the pillow. Pillow? You stare around you in total disbelief.

You're back in your room at the inn! The dream is over. And you're still alive!

You run to the window. It's morning. The sun is shining. Everything is back to normal.

You glance at the carved gargoyles. They don't look so scary. Nor does the big vegetable-oil stain on the pillow.

Wait a second. "V-vegetable oil?" you stammer. With a sickening shock, you know that everything is *not* back to normal.

You glance down at your hands and feet.

"AAAAAAAGGGHHH!" you shriek.

You escaped from the dream. But not soon enough.

You must have fallen into the fryer. Because your whole body is covered with a golden-brown crust!

You're a long, lean, extra-crispy french fry!

You've heard of "living on a shoestring." But living *as* a shoestring?

THE END

It can't be. Not him. Not here.

Hanging beside you is the Sleep Master!

The Sleep Master appears to be half human, half bat. He smiles at you with a human face. His eyes are a dead gray, almost colorless.

Chills travel up your spine. You don't know why you fear him so much. He's never done anything to you. But you can't stand to be near him.

I'm just dreaming, you remind yourself. You'd like to pinch yourself to wake up. But you don't have fingers.

"Trying to wake up?" the Sleep Master asks in a squeaky voice. "Don't bother. You're not going anywhere!"

You can't get out of the dream. But you can escape from that freaky bat-boy. All you have to do is fly away.

Then you have a strange thought. You've never talked to the Sleep Master. Maybe he can help you.

On the other hand, maybe he'll be as helpful as Attila the Hun. You hang there, trying to make up your mind.

If you try to fly away, go to PAGE 137.
If you stay and listen, go to PAGE 133.

Lord Morphos leaps in pain from your sting. "Yeow!" he bellows. Frantically, he claws at his armor. You fly out of reach.

You hear him moaning. Then you hear another sound coming from your enemy.

It's like the hiss of air escaping from a tire. Or a . . .

Balloon! you think.

The great Lord Morphos begins to shrivel, like a balloon losing air.

The Sleep Master said Lord Morphos was a big bag of wind — and it looks as if he wasn't kidding.

"Help!" Lord Morphos hisses as air rushes out of him. Soon, all that's left of him is an empty suit of armor.

Your army comes rushing up, clanking their swords in applause. Lord Morphos's army vanishes like a bad dream.

"You did it!" the Sleep Master yells. "You won!"

"Great!" you shout. "Let's go home!"

"If that's what you want," the Sleep Master replies.

Go to PAGE 21.

RING!

You nearly jump out of your skin. Do you dare answer the phone? What if *you're* on the line?

Or what if it's the Sleep Master calling? Or . . . what if it's some unknown horror?

But you can't resist.

With a shaking hand, you pick up the phone.

"Hello," answers a serious voice. "This is your dentist. I'd like you to come in this week to get your tooth pulled."

"Hooray!" you cry with relief. "My dentist! It's my dentist!"

You never thought you'd be glad to hear from your dentist. But that was before you escaped this adventure by the skin of your teeth!

THE END

R-R-R-RING!

You come awake with a rush. The phone is ringing on the table next to you. It's early morning, and everyone in the inn is still asleep. You pick up the receiver.

"Hello?" you mumble. "Hello?"

There's no one at the other end of the line.

You hang up the phone. As you do, you remember your dream.

In it, you called yourself to wake yourself up. Pretty clever, huh?

So if that was just a dream, why did your phone ring?

Are you still asleep now? Or is this really real?

Investigate further on PAGE 98.

You find yourself standing on a vast plain. It's as smooth as polished wood. The ground is broken up into black-and-white squares. With a shock, you realize it's a chessboard.

To your right and left are soldiers in white armor. You look down and see that you're wearing white armor too.

"Unbelievable!" you cry. "I said I was going to think like a chess piece. Now I *am* a chess piece — a pawn!"

The air fills with the thunder of hoofbeats. You gasp as you see a black knight on horseback. He jumps over a startled bishop and comes charging at you!

The knight's sharp lance is leveled right at your heart!

What can you do? There's no time to dream your way out.

Then you spy something at your feet. A mouse!

It's squeaking at you. Does it have a message?

You want to bend down and pick it up. But that will leave you completely unprotected from the knight's attack. He's almost on your square. What do you do?

If you raise your shield, go to PAGE 123.
If you pick up the mouse, go to PAGE 84.

Your parents can't wait. You start to climb down into the darkness.

You can't see a thing — not even your hand in front of your face. "Ow," you mutter as you poke your finger into your eye. "It's like a black hole in space!"

Just then you slip and fall. You tumble down. You brace yourself for the big splat when you hit bottom.

But, somehow, you seem to be slowing down. You drift through the blackness. Your body feels incredibly heavy. Then you hear a familiar voice.

"Mom?" you ask. "Is that you? Where are you?"

"We're in a black hole in outer space," she reveals. "You know, a collapsed star. Nothing can ever get out of here."

"A black hole?" you repeat. "Are you serious?"

"Afraid so," your dad's voice confirms sadly. "We're trapped!"

Try to escape on PAGE 37.

Only the Sleep Master can help me, you think.

You jump up and start to run after the black horse. But he's fast. Much faster than you with your two puny legs.

"It's no use," you gasp. "I'll never catch that horse." Suddenly you feel your hooves pounding over the soft turf of the hillside. You've also turned into a horse — a powerful brown horse with a white blaze on your chest. You gallop up a slope.

"This is fun!" you shout. But it comes out, *Neigh-h-h-h!*

You reach the top of the hill and scan the horizon. No sign of the black stallion. However, you spot other horses in the distance.

Hmmm. You wouldn't mind hanging out with some cool-looking horses. Do you join them?

Or do you head after the Sleep Master?

If you join the other horses, go to PAGE 13.

If you keep following the Sleep Master, go to PAGE 69.

The Sleep Master said, "Use your *noodle*," you think. Hey! It's a clue! A noodle is food. And a lunch box holds food!

You grab the lunch box and open it.

The next thing you know, you're in the tank with the giant brain. Except it's not a tank anymore. It's a gigantic pot filled with water. Hot water!

No point trying to figure out how you got here. It's a dream, remember?

A dream that's really heating up! Yeow!

You swim frantically to the side of the pot. You can't escape. The lip of the pot is out of reach!

Turn to PAGE 33.

"Doctor, come quickly!" a voice cries.

You slowly swim up through layers of sleep. You must have dozed off. But why is there a doctor here?

Suddenly you're wide awake. Your eyes snap open.

Hey! You're not in the inn — you're in a bed in a hospital!

"Wha . . ." Your voice comes out as a hoarse croak.

"Don't try to speak," the doctor cautions. "After seventy years, your throat needs to warm up."

Seventy years? Your gaze falls on your hands. The skin is wrinkled! Then you see your reflection in a mirror.

"No!" you gasp.

You're old! Your hair is gone, your face is lined with age. You open your mouth to scream.

Most of your teeth are missing!

"You've been asleep for seventy years," the doctor explains. "Your parents brought you here many years ago when they couldn't wake you up."

A wave of horror sweeps over you. The self-hypnosis worked. Too well. You've slept your life away!

The sad truth is, you're so old, you'll soon be reaching

THE END.

Suddenly you have an idea.

I can use the phone to call for help! you think. And I know just who to call!

You grab the phone and punch in a number. You hear the phone ringing on the other end. You hold your breath. Will the person you're calling answer? You feel your pulse racing. The phone rings and rings and rings. . . .

See if anyone answers on PAGE 99.

You have to do it. True, you may be trapping your parents with you. But it's a risk you have to take. Besides, they never let *you* sleep late.

"Mom," you say softly. "Dad! Come on. Wake up."

Slowly, both your parents stir. Your mom opens her eyes first and looks at you with concern.

"What's wrong?" she asks, sitting up. "Did you have a bad dream?"

"No, it wasn't a dream, it was real, and we're still in it." You try to explain. But as you talk, you have to admit to yourself that it sounds nuts. The longer you go on, the more baffled your parents look.

Finally, your dad interrupts you.

"You just had a nightmare," he declares. "Go back to bed!"

"But, Dad!" you protest.

Silently, he points to the door.

"Come on, I'll take you," your mother volunteers.

"But it was real," you tell her as she leads you away. "It still is!"

"I know, dear," she says. "It must *seem* very real."

Go to PAGE 16.

"Are you nuts?" you scream. "How can I get your stupid fries? I'm stuck under this bottle!"

"I just wanted my fries," the teenager snaps. "But forget it! And forget this stupid Buddy Burger too! It's as hard as a rock!"

He throws the burger at you. But it hits the mustard bottle, which cracks in half. Gallons of mustard start spilling out. The yellow ooze spreads over the floor. Customers and workers run for the exits, screaming.

But you're stuck under the bottle.

"Help!" you cry out. "Someone give me a hand!"

But no one's left. You're alone in Buddy Burger.

And the mustard river is starting to rise. It's already up to your ears. Your mouth is filling with it. In seconds your lungs will be flooded with the spicy stuff.

Think you're going to cut the mustard and escape?

Dream on.

THE END

That sword is too heavy for you to lift, you realize. So you grab the dagger. And you fly straight to Lord Morphos.

You fly because you've turned into a bumblebee. Lord Morphos is about a thousand times larger than you are.

But you feel cocky.

He may be the lord of the dream world, you think, but I've got a stinger!

At first Lord Morphos doesn't see you. When you buzz his helmet, he notices you.

SWOOSH!

His sword slices through the air. You easily dodge it. You're so tiny, the Eiffel Tower–sized blade seems to move in slow motion. Like a mini-missile, you swerve and zoom through a chink in Lord Morphos's armor.

Bingo! Now you're inside, next to his skin. You bury your stinger in Lord Morphos's arm.

"Take that!" you buzz.

Fly to PAGE 97.

If I rewind, you think, maybe I'll see where I went wrong.

You hit the REWIND button. But the "you" on the screen doesn't move. Instead you find yourself walking backwards to the psychoanalyst's couch and lying down again.

The door to the office opens and the psychoanalyst walks into the room — backwards! He sits in his chair, opens his mouth, and says: ".yas I tahw fo etisoppo eht yas tsuJ."

He's talking backwards! you realize. The VCR isn't rewinding the tape! It's rewinding *me*!

You begin to relive everything that's happened to you in the dream — but backwards. You run the marathon — backwards. You fly through the air as a dragon — backwards. Before you know it, you're back in the inn, holding the book in your hand — exactly where you started.

"I did it!" you shout. "I escaped from the dream!" You get up and dance for joy. Then you stop.

You didn't shout, "I escaped from the dream!" You shouted, "!maerd eht morf depacse I"

You got out of the dream, but your life is still on rewind.

All you can do is shout, "!PLEH"

DNE EHT

An extreme party? you think. No way. Things are extreme enough as is.

"Do my chores!" you order the holo-butler.

"Very good," it responds with a nod. "The first chore is to clean up. And the dirtiest thing in this house is — you!"

"Me?" you repeat dully. "But I'm not —"

"DIRT ALERT! DIRT ALERT!"

A panel in the floor slides back. Out of the hole glides a large machine. It looks like a fire hydrant with a camera mounted on top.

The machine begins to speak.

"Dirt vaporizer!" it says in a mechanical voice. "Dirt identified. Prepare to vaporize!"

"Wait a minute!" you shout. "I'm not —"

Don't wait. Go to PAGE 19.

As you lie in bed, four different pictures pop into your mind. It's as if each gargoyle is giving you a choice of a dream.

A dream that you can make come true.

In one vision, you see yourself in a castle. Maybe you'll be the ruler of a great land.

In another vision, you see yourself at school. This is your chance to do everything you always wanted to do there.

In the third vision, you see yourself as the president of a big corporation, controlling millions of dollars.

And in the last vision, you see your own home. You can turn it into anything you want.

The gargoyles wait patiently while you make up your mind. Which dream will you dream?

If you dream about your home, go to PAGE 59.

If you dream about school, go to PAGE 68.

If you dream about the castle, go to PAGE 136.

If you dream about being a millionaire, go to PAGE 15.

112

"C-c-congratulate me?" you stutter.

Something weird is going on. Everything around you — the office, the TV, the Sleep Master — seems more real now.

"Yes," the Sleep Master continues. "For waking up."

"No!" you protest. "If I woke up, how come I'm still here?"

"That's what I've been trying to tell you," he explains. "*That* was the dream. *This* is reality. Now you've proved it to yourself. You saw yourself wake up in the dream, but you're still here. Think about it. Don't you feel better now?"

Watching yourself on TV was a big mistake.

You should have watched GOOSEBUMPS instead!

THE END

You drop a pebble into the hole. Whoa! It disappears without a sound.

"That thing is *deep*!" you mutter. "I'd better get a light and see what's down there."

You gaze around. Right next to you is an oil lamp. You bend over it, trying to remember how it works.

"I need a match," you say.

"Need a match?" someone echoes.

You glance up. It's the dog gargoyle!

"You!" you shout. "You got me into this mess!"

The gargoyle flutters around, flapping its wings like a bat. Then it lands on the oil lamp and holds out a box of matches.

"Here. Need a match?" it repeats.

You reach for the box but then stop. Should you trust the gargoyle?

If you take the match, go to PAGE 22.
If you don't, go to PAGE 82.

You swagger to the principal's office.

I'll chuck out the principal and take his place, you think.

Then you stop.

There are two doors across from each other, both marked PRINCIPAL'S OFFICE. One of them has the name of the real principal on it.

The other has *your* name on it.

Which door do you go in?

If you enter the door with the real principal's name on it, go to PAGE 23.

If you enter the door with your name on it, go to PAGE 91.

The Sleep Master strides next to you. He's dressed in a running outfit, like you are. He doesn't look out of place. Except for his pointy horse ears.

"Don't give up," he urges. "You could win this thing. It's just ten more miles."

Ten miles? You can't go another step. Besides, you don't trust the Sleep Master.

But you've always wanted to win the marathon.

What do you do?

If you stop, go to PAGE 75.

If you keep running, go to PAGE 130.

"Very well," Mr. LaGamba replies meekly.

Grinning, you saunter down the hall in the direction of the cafeteria.

As you reach the steps you run into a group of kids. There's Bobby Smith, the best basketball player in school. And Cassie Green, president of the student government. They're the leaders of your school's "in crowd."

You always wanted to hang with them, but they never let you.

You're running this dream. Now's your chance to be one of the cool kids!

Then again, they were always mean to you. Why don't you blow them off? Make them squirm a little?

Across the way is another bunch of kids. There's Benny, the smartest — and nerdiest — kid in school. There's also Alicia, the queen of detention. Plus a few other losers.

You could make them popular. If you feel like it.

You can only join one group. Which do you choose?

If you join the "in crowd," go to PAGE 32.
If you join the "losers," go to PAGE 38.

You circle answer B, $E=MC^2$. You have no idea what it means. But it sure sounds smart.

RING!

"Time's up," calls out the teacher.

You hand in your paper. The teacher shakes her head. "There's no need to hand it in," she says. "Your answers were automatically recorded by our computer. I'm afraid that everyone circled the wrong answer — except one student."

She stares straight at you. "That's you!" she exclaims. "You're the only one in the entire country who circled the correct answer."

She hands you a piece of paper.

"Here is your report card," she says.

You're so surprised, you're speechless. The teacher smiles, reaches out, and shakes your shoulder.

"Wake up," she says. "You . . ."

Go to PAGE 76.

118

Bobby pokes you with his fork again. Huh? What's happening? The dream has changed. You're not sitting at the table anymore. You're *on* the table! In fact, you're sitting in a plate on Bobby's tray. You've been transformed.

But into what?

"Oooh, franks and beans!" cries Cassie. "Can I have some?"

"Sure," Bobby replies. Cassie lifts her fork over you.

You've become a plate of franks and beans!

And Bobby and Cassie are about to eat you!

I didn't ask for this dream! you think. What's the deal?

Cassie digs a fork into you. A part of you is on its way to her mouth. "Mmm." She smacks her lips. "My fave food!"

"Mine too!" Bobby agrees, swallowing some of you. Then it occurs to you. You *did* ask for this dream.

You wanted to be everyone's favorite.

And now you are.

Dog-gone it!

First Bobby eats the middle of the frank. Then Cassie finishes

THE END.

You skid into the breakfast room and sit breathlessly at your parents' table. You can't wait to get out of this creepy place!

Your dad greets you with a smile. "Good news," he announces. "Mom and I have decided to buy the inn. We're going to live here permanently!"

No!

"Isn't it wonderful?" Mom gushes.

Trembling with fear, you ask, "Guys, do you mind if I sleep in your room for the rest of my life?"

THE END

Hey! This is *my* dream, you realize. I don't have to see the principal if I don't want to!

"Inform the principal I'm busy," you tell the teacher in your snootiest voice.

Mr. LaGamba glares at you. His face slowly begins to turn red. A big vein throbs in his temple.

You hold your breath. What is he going to say? Are you about to get busted — big-time?

To find out, turn to PAGE 116.

You hit the ON/OFF button.

Instantly, the vaporizer lowers its laser. Its blinking lights go dark.

You did it! You shut it down!

You're still trembling from your close call. But at least you can relax.

"WARNING!"

A loud, booming voice makes you leap in the air.

"Electronic house program has been terminated by user!" the voice says menacingly. "House deactivation to commence now! Please vacate immediately!"

"What's happening now?" you shout. But then you see the answer. The walls and furniture around you are folding up!

You didn't only turn off the trash vaporizer. You turned off the entire house! And now it's collapsing like a pop-up book.

The wall behind you is rolling up. You'll be crushed! You spot an opening between wall and ceiling. Can you jump through — before you're turned into a pancake?

Get the results on PAGE 35.

You think about getting out of bed. Until you hear creaky noises.

"No way," you whisper. The noise and the dark are too scary. Even with the creepy headboard, you feel better staying in bed.

You lie there, trying not to look at the strange figures carved in the headboard.

You try closing your eyes tightly. No use. In your mind, the gargoyles are still staring at you.

Now you're too spooked to open your eyes. Minutes go by. It seems like you've been in this bed forever. You just keep saying to yourself, "They're not real, they're not real, they're not real. . . ."

In that case, go to PAGE 42.

"This is no time to fool around with a rodent!" you mutter angrily. You raise your shield and brace yourself.

BLANG!

It's like being hit by a freight train. Your whole body is vibrating. You can't survive another hit like that one.

But the knight is turning back in your direction.

Oh, no. Here he comes.

You lamely hold up your shield. And the black knight promptly splits it into two with his lance.

Spurring his horse, the knight gallops at you full tilt. The lance is coming closer every second. As you prepare to meet your doom, you think:

This is one knight I'll never forget!

THE END

"I used my noodle. . . . I used my noodle. . . ."

The pillow under your head is soft and warm. Slowly, you open your eyes. You're back where you started, in the bedroom at the inn. And it's daytime.

You did it! You beat Lord Morphos. As promised, he returned you to reality. Your reality.

Happily, you jump out of bed and run to your parents' room. But something stops you in your tracks. It's your reflection in the mirror.

Your head. It's still the size of a beach ball!

"NOOOO!" you cry. With your new, powerful brain, you try to think of something to get your head back to normal. But it's hopeless. You're safe back in your own reality. But your head is stuck like this — for good.

Explaining this to your family is going to be one big headache!

THE END

Beads of sweat roll off your forehead. Suddenly the Sleep Master appears next to you.

"It's simple," he whispers. "Use your noodle!"

"Great advice!" you sneer. "How about a computer?"

Then you notice something on the floor. An old plastic lunch box.

In spite of your problems, you can't help wondering what's inside.

But this isn't the time to think about food.

Or is it?

If you try to think even harder, go to PAGE 71.

If you check out what's in the lunch box, go to PAGE 103.

You take a deep breath and circle answer A.

HONK!

A minivan speeds by, just missing you. A few of your feathers go fluttering off on the wind.

Feathers?

You glance down at yourself — and almost faint. You've been transformed into a chicken! And you're in the middle of a road. Cars whiz by in both directions. A Cadillac is heading right at you.

"Bu-u-u-uck!" you screech as you flap your wings. Frantically, you run for your life.

This is no joke! you realize. If I die in this dream, I'll be dead meat for real!

Desperately, you try to cross the road. Your little feet don't move very fast. But you reach the next lane.

HONK! The blare of a truck's horn shatters the air. You glance up. A gigantic eighteen-wheeler is barreling down on you. You get a flash of insight.

The true answer to the question is . . .

The chicken never made it across the road!

THE END

"Let's party!" you shout, jumping off the couch.

"Very good," your holo-butler says with a nod. "I will invite the guests and have the servo-kitchen prepare immense quantities of snacks. Please prepare yourself."

Prepare myself? you wonder. For what?

Just then one wall of the room becomes a giant loudspeaker. "What a cool sound system!" you cry.

Then the sound comes on.

With the force of a hurricane, the sound from the speaker knocks you to the floor! The music is so loud, it feels as if your whole body is shaking apart.

You scream in pain. But you can't hear your own screams over the noise.

Forget calling the computer. It couldn't hear you, either.

This is what the holo-butler meant when it said prepare yourself, you realize. There must be earplugs somewhere.

But it's too late now. The sound is literally killing you — and there's nothing you can do.

Before choosing this path, you could have used some sound advice!

THE END

Even though you're already scared, you can't resist a GOOSEBUMPS book. This book is too good to read down here. You want to snuggle up with it in your room.

You go upstairs and jump into bed. Warm under the thick blanket, you feel drowsy.

But you've got to try to read this great story.

You open the book.

Go to PAGE 1.

"Test?" you cry.

How can you take a test? You haven't studied at all. You don't even know what the test is about!

"Hey, I don't want to take a test," you begin to protest.

"Shhh!" The principal puts his fingers to his lips. "They're about to start. Hurry up, your seat is over there!"

All the other students are already seated, hunched over their papers, pencils in hand. Reluctantly you walk to the front. Taking tests always makes you nervous.

"Psst!"

A kid at a desk is trying to get your attention. It's Al Wheeler, the smartest guy in your class.

"Hey," he whispers. "This test's a killer. But I already wrote down the answers." He holds out a piece of paper. "Want to see them?"

This is your chance to get all the right answers. But it's cheating. What do you do?

If you take the paper, go to PAGE 31.
If you keep walking, go to PAGE 50.

The excitement of the cheering people, the runners, and the feel of your feet hitting the ground has you psyched. You always wanted to run in the marathon. And now you're doing it!

Even if this is just a dream, it's a great dream.

"Okay," you pant to the Sleep Master, "I'm going for it!"

The next thing you know, you're in first place. All the other runners look exhausted. But you're no longer even breathing hard. You decide to run faster. Your feet fly over the pavement.

There's the finish line! You hear the crowd cheering as you break the tape. You did it! You won the New York City Marathon! The race officials run up to you.

"Congratulations!" they shout. "And here's your prize — ten billion dollars!"

Celebrate on PAGE 11.

"He won't fool me," you declare. "I'm going to get rid of him — once and for all."

You open your mouth and breathe a fireball at the plane. It disappears in a burst of flames. "Good-bye, dream boy," you chuckle.

You are one happy dragon. No more Sleep Master. No more bad dreams!

Now all you have to do is wake up.

Come on, get up, you tell yourself.

You open your eyes and . . .

See what's on PAGE 57.

"I'll stay!" you declare.

"All hail the ruler of the dream world!"

Your faithful servant, the Sleep Master, calls out this command. Your army bows down before you. You ride your beautiful white steed toward your castle on the distant hill.

"What is your wish?" asks the Sleep Master. Hmmm. You can do anything you want — fly a jet plane, be a movie star, explore the deepest oceans. As you consider the possibilities, a fleeting memory crosses your mind.

"That's odd," you say to the Sleep Master. "I just recalled a funny dream I had. I was an ordinary kid, on vacation with my parents. We were staying in an inn by the ocean. And I was scared to fall asleep."

The Sleep Master opens his mouth as if he's about to say something. But doesn't.

"Unbelievable," you laugh. "Imagine me, ruler of the dream world, just an ordinary kid. What a life!"

You and the Sleep Master have a good laugh. Then the two of you ride off to your castle.

THE END

You're about to drop off the cave ceiling and fly away. But you stop yourself.

Something is different about this dream. It's the first dream in which you *know* you are inside a dream.

Something's going on. You have to find out what — even if it means talking to *him.*

"Okay," you agree. "Go ahead. I'm listening."

The next thing you know, you're a human kid again. You and the Sleep Master are standing on the tower of a grim castle on a windswept plain. Now the Sleep Master is a young boy about your age. He wears a brown cloak.

"I was once like you," he explains. "I was a kid, living in the other world — the world you think is the real world. But one night I fell asleep. In my dream, I came to this world. I turned into what you see now. A spirit — the Sleep Master. And I have never been able to get back."

"Why can't you get back?" you ask.

But you're afraid to hear the answer.

Find out on PAGE 14.

You jab the button marked ALARM.

BZZZZ!

The annoying sound of the alarm clock makes you groan. You roll over in bed.

In bed! You jerk upright and force your eyes open.

Yes! You're back at the inn!

You made it! Somehow you escaped from the dream.

But, hey, it was only a dream. Right? Even if it seemed real.

You leap out of bed. There they are — four gargoyles, carved in the headboard. They don't look scary in the daylight.

You chuckle to yourself. As if these wooden creatures could be real! What a joke!

You pull on your sneakers and head for the door.

Then you stop.

Did one of the gargoyles move? Did it smile at you? You run downstairs as fast as you can. Behind you, you hear what sounds like the flapping of wings in your room.

Turn to PAGE 119.

"Let's go to the soccer game," you cry. "We'll show those jocks we belong there too."

The kids all look at you with admiration. All except Benny. He seems doubtful.

You give Benny some encouragement. "Come on, Benny. You don't want to be a nerd all your life," you tell him.

You lead the way to the athletic field.

"Gee," Alicia says to you, "do you play soccer?"

"Sure. I'm great at this game," you brag. Actually, you don't even know how many players are on a side. "In fact, I wish I could play right now."

The next thing you know, you're running down the field, deftly dribbling the ball. You're in the game! What a rush!

A player on the opposing team tries to steal the ball. But with a quick move, you spin and slip the tackle.

The goal is just ahead. The goalie has his hands up, waving. He's trying to distract you, you think.

Then a teammate runs beside you, shouting, "Pass the ball."

You hesitate. Should you pass the ball or shoot?

If you shoot, go to PAGE 48.
If you pass, go to PAGE 81.

136

You gaze up in awe at the castle in front of you. Twin towers soar above the drawbridge, guarding the entrance.

A real castle! You've been transported to some medieval kingdom! You're sure you'll meet knights and lords and ladies. Excellent!

Maybe I'll fight a dragon, you think. Or an evil wizard!

You race up the path toward the massive wooden gates. But as you approach, you slow down. The place seems deserted. Where is everyone?

Then you spot a dark figure in the shadows under the entrance archway. You rush toward it. You're about to shout out a greeting — when the figure steps out of the shadows. Your words stick in your throat.

"Oh, no!" you cry in dismay.

Now you know where you are. This is terrible! Worse than terrible!

You're in . . .

Where? Find out on PAGE 49.

Frantically, you drop from the ceiling and speed for the cave's mouth. You burst into the dark night. Free! You got away from the Sleep Master!

"Yeah!" you shout.

At the same moment, you're shoved hard against the seat behind you.

"What?" you cry in surprise. Without warning, you're piloting a jet fighter, roaring across the sky!

What happened? A moment ago you were a bat. Now you're a jet pilot?

Then you realize — it's a dream! Things can change in the blink of an eye.

You grab the controls. Somehow you know exactly how to fly the thundering jet. "This dream rules!" you shout.

A burst of machine gunfire explodes from behind your plane. You peek over your shoulder.

Uh-oh.

The Sleep Master is chasing you in a jet fighter of his own.

Zoom to PAGE 83.

About R.L. Stine

R.L. Stine is the most popular author in America. He is the creator of the *Goosebumps*, *Give Yourself Goosebumps*, *Fear Street*, and *Ghosts of Fear Street* series, among other popular books. He has written more than 200 scary novels for kids. Bob lives in New York City with his wife, Jane, teenage son, Matt, and dog, Nadine.